The Arabian Nights

This Books Belongs To

- -

Wonder House

Printed 2022

(An imprint of Prakash Books Pvt. Ltd.)

Wonder House Books
Corporate & Editorial Office
113-A, 1st Floor, Ansari Road,
Daryaganj, New Delhi-110002
Tel +91 11 2324 7062-65

ISBN : 978-93-5440-535-8

Printed in India

Contents

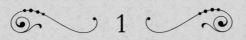

1

1001 Nights

*T*his is the story of Scheherazade, the greatest storyteller there ever was. She lived in a time when the ruler of the land bore a terrible grudge against women. His name was Shahryar.

Shahryar had a wife whom he loved more than anyone else. But she betrayed him.

Shahryar called his minister and had his wife executed. He then passed a law in the land that he would take a bride every day and have her executed the next morning. This way, his bride would never be able to betray him.

The people of the land begged him to rethink this terrible law. But Shahryar was relentless.

Each morning, a bride would get executed. In the end, there was hardly any woman left in the city of marriageable age. One day, the minister could not find a bride for the sultan.

He had two daughters, Scheherazade and Dunyazad. Scheherazade, the eldest, was very well read.

Scheherazade soon realised that the sultan would have her father executed if he failed to bring a bride that night. She told her father, "Take me to the sultan. I shall be his bride. Either my wisdom will save me and the daughters of this land or I shall die like others in vain."

That night, when Shahryar lifted the veil of his bride, he saw Scheherazade's beautiful but sorrowful eyes. "Is there any way I can lessen your pain?" he asked.

Scheherazade already had a plan. "I am missing my sister Dunyazad," she said. "I want to see her one last time." Shahryar immediately sent for her sister.

Dunyazad slept with her sister that night and, as instructed by her sister, woke early next morning. She said, "Oh Scheherazade! Won't you tell me one of your wonderful stories one last time?" Scheherazade coyly said, "I will with pleasure, only if the sultan permits."

Shahryar consented, and so began Scheherazade's first story of 1001 nights.

2

Aladdin and the Magic Lamp

Aladdin was a good-for-nothing boy. His father had died and his mother worked hard to make a living. One day, a stranger came to him and said, "I am your uncle. Take me to your mother." Aladdin's mother was astonished for Aladdin had no uncle. The stranger, who was actually a magician, gave them some money and said, "I could not do anything for my brother but I want to give Aladdin a good life."

Some days later, he took Aladdin to a desolate valley. There, he threw some powder on the ground and a square stone with a brass ring at its center appeared out of nowhere.

The magician said, "Pull the stone by the ring and go down the pathway. You will enter a hall. At the end of it, you will find a lamp burning in a nook. Bring it to me." He gave Aladdin a ring and told him that it would keep him safe.

Aladdin went down the pathway and found himself in a large hall filled with treasure. He filled his pockets with some precious gemstones. Then he took the lamp and came right back.

"I have the lamp, uncle, take me out," shouted Aladdin.

"Hand me the lamp, son," the magician shouted back.

When Aladdin refused to part with the lamp, the magician grew angry. He closed the opening of the pathway and was gone. Aladdin cried for help but in vain. As he was wiping away his tears, he chanced to rub the ring on his finger.

The next instant, a huge genie stood before him. "What can I do for you, master?" he asked.

"Please take me home," said Aladdin.

Within seconds, he was standing inside his house. He told his mother everything about the secret place and how the magician had left him to die. Aladdin's mother was glad to have her son back. Slowly, she sold the gemstones and they lived happily for a long time.

One day, his mother was cleaning the lamp. As she rubbed it, a genie appeared in front of her. "What can I do for you, master?" roared the genie.

"We are hungry, bring us something to eat," said Aladdin.

In a moment, the table was covered with all sorts of delicious foods in plates of gold and silver. The genie fulfilled all their wishes and they became rich over time and lived happily in a beautiful house.

3

From Rags to Riches

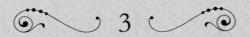

One day, when Aladdin was walking past the sultan's palace, he happened to see the princess and instantly decided to marry her. He told his mother, "Take the gemstones that I had brought back from the cave to the sultan. I am sure he will not refuse your request."

Next day, Aladdin's mother went to the palace and said, "Sultan, my son wishes to marry the princess and he sends these gemstones as a token of gratitude."

The sultan had never seen such rare and beautiful jewels. He said, "Tell your son to send me forty large golden vessels full

of jewels that you have given me. Remember, each vessel must be brought by a black slave followed by a white slave, all richly dressed."

When Aladdin heard this, he rubbed his magic lamp and summoned the genie. He told him to bring all that the sultan had demanded. In the blink of an eye, the genie granted his wish.

When Aladdin's mother went to the sultan, he could not believe his eyes. He immediately consented to the marriage.

Aladdin was happy and commanded the genie to make his wedding the grandest in the kingdom.

The sultan was charmed by Aladdin and his riches. Aladdin expressed his desire before the genie to build a palace fit for the princess before he married her.

Next morning, a palace stood right before, rivalling in grandeur, the sultan's palace.

The marriage then took place with much aplomb.

4

The Happy Ending

$\mathcal{A}$laddin and the princess lived in happiness for quite some time before tragedy struck.

With his magic, the magician had found out that the lamp was still with Aladdin. He dressed as a peddler of lamps and went about town, crying, "Who wants new lamps for old ones?"

Aladdin was out hunting. So, the princess said to her maid, "Take this old lamp and exchange it for a new one."

The magician gave a shining new lamp to the maid and made off with the magic lamp. He rubbed it and instantly the genie appeared.

"Carry Aladdin's palace to Africa," commanded the magician. The genie did as commanded.

Next day, the sultan was shocked to find Aladdin's palace missing. At once, he ordered his men to bring Aladdin back from the hunt. "Where is my daughter? Bring her back or

I shall have you beheaded," thundered the sultan when his son-in-law returned.

Aladdin left the city to look for his princess. His search was futile and losing all hope, he started crying. Suddenly, the ring on his finger rubbed against his cheek and the genie of the ring appeared. Relieved, Aladdin said, "Genie, take me to the place where my princess is." When the princess saw Aladdin, she told him about her foolishness.

Together, Aladdin and the princess poisoned the magician and returned home with the genie's help. The whole town rejoiced on their return.

5

Sinbad and the Monster Bird

There once lived in the city of Baghdad a merchant named Sinbad. He was a fearless sailor who made adventurous voyages across great seas. On one such voyage, he reached a beautiful but lonely island. After exploring it, Sinbad went off to sleep. When he woke up, he found the ship gone and with it, all his hopes of returning to Baghdad.

Roaming the island aimlessly, Sinbad climbed up a tall tree to look for any signs of humans. He saw a strange spherical object far away. Hoping to find a secret door on it, he ran towards it. But he found none, so he waited beside it.

When evening came, the sky suddenly became very dark. Sinbad looked up and saw the shadow of a giant bird descending upon the spherical object which was its egg. He saw this as his only chance to escape from the island. He tied himself to the giant bird's claw and waited patiently.

Early next morning, the bird took flight and Sinbad found himself in a mountainous region full of lava and volcanoes. The bird flew over them and landed in a deep ravine. Sinbad quickly untied himself from the bird and hid behind a rock. He looked around and saw that the ravine was surrounded on all sides by steep walls. And at the bottom of the pit were enormous snakes!

Wait! The snakes were not the only astonishing thing there. The rocky terrain was encrusted with huge diamonds! Sinbad remained hidden inside a cave all night. At daybreak, he trudged his way out of the cave only to see huge chunks of meat raining down from the sky!

Sinbad remembered stories of merchants who would drop pieces of meat into the Valley of Diamonds with the hope that the precious stones would get stuck to them. Then, they would wait for the eagles to swoop down on the diamond-studded pieces of meat and carry them to their nests. Later, the merchants would climb up to their nests and shoo away the birds to get the diamonds.

Sinbad quickly filled his pockets with as many diamonds as he could and tied himself with his turban to a piece of meat. When the eagles swooped down to pick up the meat, Sinbad went off with them.

When the merchants came by a nest and found a man instead of diamonds, they were shocked and angry. Sinbad assured them that his pockets were full of diamonds and he was ready to share them.

The merchants were happy with the deal and promised Sinbad a place in their ship to return safely to Baghdad.

On reaching Baghdad, Sinbad sold his diamonds for a great fortune, and promised himself never to return to sea again.

6

Sultan Sindbad and His Falcon

Sultan Sindbad had a pet falcon who accompanied him wherever he went. She had a golden cup around her neck.

One day, the falcon told the sultan that it was a good day to hunt. So the sultan set out with his hunting troop. A gazelle got trapped in the net laid by the sultan's men. He asked his men not to let the gazelle escape. The frightened gazelle moved towards the sultan, jumped over his head and escaped.

The sultan then took upon himself to catch the gazelle and decided not to return till he had done so. Taking the falcon with him, he rode out on his horse in search of the gazelle.

Soon he was upon the gazelle. The falcon swooped down and blinded the gazelle with her sharp claws. The sultan then killed the gazelle with his mace, stripped its skin and put it across the horse's saddle. He then retraced his steps to his troops.

But all the hard work had made the sultan thirsty. He looked for water but there was no sign of water anywhere. Eventually, he came upon a tree that was dripping some kind of liquid on the forest floor. Mistaking it for water, the sultan took the cup from the falcon's neck and held it under the tree to collect some liquid. Just as he placed the cup in front of the falcon, she overturned it. He filled the cup again and put it before the horse. The falcon overturned it again.

This made Sultan Sindbad very angry and he cut off the falcon's wings. The falcon gave out a cry of anguish and looked up at the tree. Following her gaze, Sultan Sindbad looked up and saw a brood of vipers. He realised that the dripping liquid was poison from their mouths. The falcon was merely protecting her sultan. The falcon died in pain, leaving the remorseful sultan to regret his foolish action.

7

The Tale of the Bull and the Ass

$\mathcal{L}$ong ago, there lived a farmer who had an amazing gift, He could understand the language of animals. He had a bull and an ass who helped him in his work. The bull would toil and plough the fields all day long. The ass would carry goods to the market in the evening and rest all day.

One day, the ass was speaking with the bull in a low voice. The farmer saw them and hid behind a tree to listen. The ass said, "You work hard all day but eat only once. I eat and rest

the whole day. Don't you think our master is being harsh on you?" "True, my friend! But I cannot betray my master," the bull replied sadly.

The ass suggested that the bull should pretend to be sick the next day and rest. The bull liked the idea. When the farmer heard this, he decided to teach them a lesson.

The next day, the bull pretended to be sick. The farmer allowed him to rest and dragged the ass to the field.

The ass had to work hard all day and was exhausted by evening. When he returned, the bull said, "I shall pretend to be sick and rest tomorrow as well."

"No! No!" cried the ass. "Our master was upset with my work today. If you do not go to work tomorrow, he will sell you to a butcher."

The bull got scared and decided not to pretend anymore. "We should be sincere with our work," the ass added.

The farmer was glad to hear this.

8

The Greedy Merchant

Abdullah was a rich but greedy merchant. One day, he loaded his forty camels with costly spices and set out on a business trip. On his way back, he stopped at an inn to rest. There, he met a holy man who informed him about a secret land with hidden treasure.

"You can load your camels with precious jewels but you must give me half of them," said the holy man. Abdullah agreed immediately.

The holy man took Abdullah to a land surrounded by lofty mountains. There, he sprinkled some mysterious powder on the ground.

Suddenly, there arose clouds of smoke and Abdullah saw an opening in a mountain which led to a cave full of treasure.

Abdullah quickly filled all his bags with the treasure and loaded them onto the camels. The holy man asked Abdullah to leave behind twenty camels loaded with riches as his share.

Abdullah said, "You are a holy man. Why do you need so much wealth? You can keep ten camels." The holy man understood that Abdullah was being greedy but he agreed.

Not satisfied, Abdullah said, "Ten camels would be a burden to you. I'll take them with me." This made the holy man very annoyed.

As he prepared to leave, Abdullah asked him to give the box of mysterious powder as well. The holy man decided to teach Abdullah a lesson. He warned, "You can take the powder but remember–if you rub it on your left eye, you will see the hidden treasures. But if you rub it on your right eye, you will go blind." So saying, the holy man went away.

Abdullah ignored the holy man's advice and immediately rubbed some powder on his left eye. His excitement knew no bounds as he could see more hidden treasures in the mountains! But his greed got the better of him and he rubbed some powder on his right eye as well. At once, he went completely blind. It was too late to repent.

9

The Ropemaker

Abu Hassan was a poor ropemaker. He would sell ropes in the market and earn just enough to feed his family.

Abu had two friends who were rich. One day, they gave him hundred gold coins and said, "Buy a shop with this money and start a business. We will meet you after six months."

Abu thanked his friends and decided to buy some sweets for his sons first. He took out ten gold coins and hid the remaining ninety coins in his turban. He wore the turban and went to the market.

There he bought a box of sweets for his kids. On his way home, suddenly, a kite swooped down and grabbed the box of sweets. But Abu did not let go of it. The relentless kite then pulled at his turban and flew away with it. Abu watched the kite fly away in dismay. Abu Hassan was poor again.

Six months later, when Abu's friends visited him, they were upset to see him in the same state. "This time we will give you something worthless and see how you use it to become

rich." Saying so, they gave him a piece of lead and left.

One day, a fisherman, asked him for a piece of lead to tie to his fishing net. Abu gladly gave away the piece of lead. The fisherman promised to give him the first fish he caught in return.

As promised, the fisherman gave Abu a big fish. When Abu cut open the fish, he found a big shining diamond inside. He sold it and bought a shop with that money. He started selling silk and became a rich man.

When his friends visited him again after six months, they were happy to find him rich.

10

The Enchanted Horse

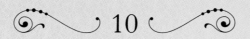

Once an Indian traveller visited the kingdom of Shiraz in Persia. He presented the sultan with a beautiful wooden horse that could fly anywhere.

The sultan was pleased and offered to buy it. The traveller said, "O sultan! I'll give you my horse if you let me marry your daughter."

The sultan's son Prince Firoz was furious to hear this and said, "Let me test the horse, before you buy it, father."

The impatient prince then mounted the horse and before the traveller could instruct him, he took flight. The sultan blamed the traveller for the crisis and put him behind bars till his son's safe return.

In the meanwhile, Prince Firoz reached the kingdom of Bengal. There he landed in the palace of the princess of Bengal and fell in love with her. The sultan of Bengal consented to their marriage. Prince Firoz then flew to Persia with his princess on the enchanted horse.

Upon his son's safe return, the sultan released the traveller. But the traveller wanted to take revenge. He tricked the guards one night and fled with the princess of Bengal on his enchanted horse. When they were flying over the valley of Kashmir, the princess saw a palace and started shouting for help. The sultan of Kashmir came to the princess's rescue.

He made the horse come down and had the traveller beheaded. The princess, however, was in trouble still as the king of Kashmir planned to marry her. But the princess could not forget her love for Prince Firoz. So she started acting like a mad woman, seeing this the sultan called the doctors to cure her.

Prince Firoz, in the meantime, had left Persia in search of his beloved. He eventually reached Kashmir. When he heard the story of the mad princess, he realized that it must

be his lost love. He went to the sultan's court disguised as a learned doctor.

Alone with the princess, the prince revealed his identity and together they planned their escape. As planned, the enchanted horse was placed in the city square and the princess sat on it. The sultan and his courtiers watched as the prince lit a coal fire. Soon, thick smoke engulfed the horse. At once, the prince mounted it and flew off with his princess. It was too late for anyone to understand anything.

The Sultan of Persia was delighted to see the prince and his princess, and announced a grand wedding for them.

11

Three Wise Men and the Camel

There lived in Arabia a man who had a camel. One day, his camel was lost. The man searched for it everywhere, but in vain.

Then he came across three wise men, and asked, "Has any one of you seen my camel?"

The first wise man asked, "Is your camel blind in one eye?"

"Yes, my camel is blind in one eye," the man replied.

Then the second wise man asked, "Does your camel have a deformed leg?"

The man responded, "Yes, he is lame!"

The third wise man then enquired, "Was your camel carrying honey on one side and grain on the other?"

The man pleaded, "If you have seen my camel, which I know you have, please tell me where it is."

But the three wise men replied, "No! We have never laid eyes on your camel."

This angered the man and he said, "How do you know so much about my camel if you have never set your eyes upon him?"

Saying so, he took the three wise men to the sultan to seek justice.

When the sultan heard the man's story, he turned to the three wise men and asked, "How do all of you know so much about his camel when you have never seen it?"

The first man said, "When I passed the pastures, I found that only one side was neatly eaten. So I guessed that the camel must be blind in one eye."

The second man said, "I noticed that the hoof marks of the camel were deeper on one side than the other. So I assumed

that the camel must be lame."

The third man said, "I saw grains and honey scattered on either side of the pathway. So I guessed that the camel was carrying grains on one side and honey on the other."

The sultan was amazed at their wisdom and said, "They are not thieves, but wisest of all men. Go and look for your camel on the path they have travelled, and you shall find it."

And to the three wise men, the sultan said, "Be my ministers and help me rule my kingdom, wisely."

12

Ali Baba and the Forty Thieves:
Treasure in a Cave

*T*here once lived a poor man in Persia named Ali Baba. His brother Cassim was a rich man.

One day, Ali Baba was chopping wood in the forest. Suddenly, he heard a distant rumbling sound. It was made by a band of forty horsemen. Quickly, he climbed a tree, hiding his logs-laden donkeys behind bushes.

The horsemen came to a halt beneath the tree where Ali Baba was hiding. Then a man who looked like their leader

approached a cave and shouted, "Open Sesame!" At once, the rock in front of the cave shifted and the forty horsemen went inside it.

After a while, all the horsemen came out. The leader then faced the cave and shouted, "Close Sesame!" Immediately, the rock shifted once again and closed the cave opening.

The robbers, for the horsemen were indeed robbers, then mounted their horses and went away.

It was almost dark. Ali Baba descended the tree and, out of curiosity, shouted at the rock, "Open, Sesame!" The rock moved and gave way to the cave.
Ali Baba went in cautiously.

Inside the cave were riches fit for a sultan's treasury. Heaps of gold and silver, bales of silk, and uncountable money! The robbers kept their loot in the cave.

Ali Baba loaded his donkeys with as much gold as he could and left the cave. "Close, Sesame!" he said. The cave door closed. Ali Baba went towards home.

Once home, he quickly shut the door and unloaded the gold for his wife to see. "Where have you been?" asked his wife.

Ali Baba narrated the whole story and added, "Keep it a secret. Now let us bury the gold."

"I shall not tell anyone, but let me count the gold before you bury it," pleaded his wife. "I shall go to Cassim's wife and borrow a measure, to weigh the gold." Ali Baba agreed.

Cassim's wife shrewdly thought, "I have to know what poor Ali Baba has brought home." She put some glue underneath the measure.

When Ali Baba's wife returned the measure to Cassim's wife, she was dumbstruck to find a gold coin stuck to the measure.

"Ali Baba is unimaginably rich!" she told Cassim. "What are you talking about?" Cassim asked, bewildered.

His wife then narrated the whole story and asked Cassim to go and find out from Ali Baba, about his newly acquired wealth.

13

Ali Baba and the Forty Thieves:
Trapped!

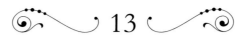

*E*arly next morning, Cassim reached Ali Baba's house and said, "You feign poverty, but your wife measures gold with scales! My clever wife had put glue at the bottom of the measure. A gold coin was stuck to it."

Ali Baba had no choice but to tell him the whole story. He also told him the way to the cave and the phrase that opened it.

Before dawn Cassim went to the forest and, standing in front of the rock, exclaimed, "Open Sesame". The cave opened and Cassim rushed in. The door closed behind him instantly.

He began loading the gold into sacks. But in his excitement, he forgot the phrase that opened the door. He was trapped!

Soon the robbers returned. Upon entering, they found poor Cassim with the sacks of gold and slayed him. They cut his body in four parts and hung them at the door inside the cave.

Meanwhile, when Cassim did not return, his wife became worried and went to Ali Baba. Ali Baba came to the forest to look for Cassim.

When Ali Baba reached the cave, he saw Cassim's hanging body. He quickly took down the body, loaded it on his donkey and headed home.

When he reached Cassim's house, he told Morgina, the house-help, "Morgina, your master is dead. Arrange for his proper burial, but let no one know how he died."

Morgina went to Baba Mustafa, an old tailor, and gave him a few gold coins. She then blindfolded him and brought him to Cassim's house. There, he sewed Cassim's body parts together.

Morgina then took him back blindfolded and gave him few more gold coins.

Meanwhile, when the robbers saw that Cassim's body was stolen, they knew that they had been discovered. One of the robbers went off to the village to enquire about any mysterious death in recent past. After a while, he came across Baba Mustafa who helped him reach Cassim's house.

The robber then marked a cross on the door and left to return with full force.

14

Ali Baba and the Forty Thieves:
Look Out Ali Baba

When Morgina saw her master's door marked, she became suspicious. She took a chalk and marked all the other doors in the vicinity with the same sign. Thus, the robber's ploy was foiled by clever Morgina.

The leader of the robbers then took it upon himself to meet Baba Mustafa and identify the house.

"I have a brilliant plan of revenge. Bring me twenty mules and forty large oil jars. Fill only one of the jars with oil," the

leader ordered. He instructed his thirty-nine men to hide in the empty jars with their weapons.

The leader then mounted his horse and led the twenty mules, each loaded with two jars into the village. It was already dark when the robbers reached Cassim's house.

"I have travelled a long way. Can I stay the night in your house, kind man?" asked the leader.

Ali Baba failed to recognise the robber in his disguise and obliged readily.

He summoned Morgina and said, "Get the mules unloaded and put the oil jars in the garden. Then, prepare dinner for our guest."

Morgina did as she was told. In the kitchen, the cook Abdalla said, "We are running short of oil. How will I make dinner?"

"There are forty jars of oil in our garden. Don't worry, I'll go and fetch some for you." Saying so, Morgina took the oil can from the kitchen and went into the garden. The moment she tried opening the lid of the first jar, she heard a voice from inside ask, "Is it time, master?"

Morgina kept her calm and changing her voice said, "Not yet." She then went to each jar one by one, and from all the jars except one that contained oil, came the same question. Morgina gave the same answer to each. She now knew that Ali Baba had unknowingly let in forty robbers into the house, and their leader was sitting with him in merriment.

15

Ali Baba and the Forty Thieves:
Ali Baba is Rich

Morgina kept her calm. She filled her can with oil from the only oil jar that there was, and boiled it. She took Abdalla's help and poured the boiling oil on each of the men hiding in the jars. The robbers burned to death.

Unaware that his men have died, the leader came into the garden when everybody was asleep. He called his men to come out of the jars but no one replied. When he opened the lids of the jars, he was shocked to find all his men charred to death. Fearing for his life, the leader of the robbers fled.

In the morning when Ali Baba woke up, Morgina took him to the garden. She showed him the dead robbers and narrated what had transpired in the darkness of the night.

"Morgina, you saved my life. I shall remain forever indebted to you," said Ali Baba.

Now, the leader of the robbers wanted to avenge the death of his men. Disguised as Kazia Hussain, a cloth merchant, he befriended Ali Baba.

One day, Ali Baba invited Kazia Hussain to dinner. "I cannot partake any meal at your place son, as I do not take salt in my meals," Hussain tried to excuse himself.

But Ali Baba said, "I shall ask my cook not to put salt in your meal." Hussain agreed to come.

When Morgina saw the new guest, she immediately recognised him as the leader of the robbers. Morgina then requested her master to allow for a dance performance as a present for his esteemed guest.

During the performance, as Kazia Hussain watched in rapt attention, Morgina took out a dagger and stabbed his heart.

"What have you done, Morgina!" Ali Baba cried in horror. Morgina disclosed the identity of the robber and Ali Baba thanked her for saving his life. "I wish to make you my daughter-in-law," Ali Baba told Morgina. She soon wedded Ali Baba's son.

After a year, Ali Baba visited the cave and realised that apart from him nobody was aware of its existence. He had riches beyond measure and had no one to fear.

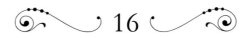

16

The Demon Who Loved to Hear Stories

Once there lived a wealthy merchant. He made his fortune travelling and selling goods. On one such journey, he stopped to rest in an orchard. As he rested, he ate some dates and threw the kernels carelessly.

Suddenly, a demon stood before him with a drawn sword and growled, "I will kill you, O Merchant!" Aghast, the merchant asked, "O Mighty One, what is my crime?"

The demon said, "One of the kernels that you so carelessly threw has killed my son. I am going to avenge his death."

The merchant knew his end was near, so he pleaded, "Let me go home to my family one last time, I promise to return after a year." The demon agreed.

The merchant went home and took care of his family affairs. After a year, he left home and returned to the orchard.

While the merchant was waiting for the demon, three old men came by. They had a deer and two black hounds with them. Seeing the merchant, they asked, "What brings you here? Do you not know that this place is full of demons and beasts?"

The merchant then told the men the story of his misfortune. Just then, the demon arrived with a drawn sword.

One of the old men who had a deer, stepped forward and asked the demon. "If I tell you a story more bizarre than the story of this merchant and you, will you spare a third of this merchant's life?" The demon loved to hear stories, so he agreed.

The old man then narrated how his deer was actually his cousin to whom he was married. She turned into a deer as a punishment for her cunningness.

The demon was pleased with the story and pardoned a third of the merchant's life.

The second old man who had two black hounds said, "I will tell you a story more unusual than this, will you spare another third of this merchant's life?" The demon agreed again.

The man then told the demon that the two black hounds were actually his brothers. They had been doomed to remain as hounds for the rest of their lives because of their unbrotherly act. The demon pardoned another third of the merchant's life.

The third old man put the same question before the demon and then told him that the mule accompanying him was actually his wife. The demon was surprised and granted the remaining third of the merchant's life.

Thus, the three men saved the merchant's life, and parted their ways with a happy heart and mind.

17

The Fisherman and the Genie

Once, there lived an old fisherman with his wife and three children. The poor chap would go fishing everyday in the hope of catching a big fish and earning a lot of money. One day, while he was fishing, he felt a heavy weight in his net. His eyes lit up at the thought that he has caught a big fish. But to his dismay, he found the carcass of an ass in the net.

The fisherman cast his net again and waited patiently. But again all that he could gather was either mud or waste. All his efforts had gone in vain and he became worried, "What will I feed my family today?"

Having lost all his hopes, the fisherman cast his net for one last time and waited. When he pulled the net, it felt heavy again. "This seems to be a big catch!" he thought in excitement. But instead of a fish, he found a yellow jar in the net that was sealed with a beautiful lid. He opened the lid

with the hope of finding something precious inside. To his surprise, a thick smoke rose from the jar and took the shape of a genie.

The fisherman fell back with fear. The genie laughed wickedly and said, "I have been hungry for ages. Bring me some food or I shall kill you."

"But why would you kill me?" cried the fisherman. "I freed you from this jar."

The wicked genie would hear nothing. The fisherman was at his wits end but he gathered courage and asked, "O Genie, before I die, I wish to know how a huge genie such as you could fit into this small jar!"

The haughty genie laughed and began to change himself to smoke and entered the jar.

"Do you believe me now?" asked a voice from inside the jar. The fisherman lost no time and immediately shut the jar and threw it back into the sea. He sighed deeply as he picked his net and returned home. He was happy that his presence of mind had helped him save his life.

The Tale of the Hunchback

In the city of Basra, there lived a tailor and his wife. Once, they went to see a hunchback's performance. They liked the performance so much that they invited the hunchback to supper. The tailor's wife prepared a delicious meal but while eating, a fishbone got stuck in the hunchback's throat and he choked on it. The couple feared that they might have killed the hunchback. Quickly, they wrapped him in a cloth and left him at a doctor's doorstep.

The doctor stumbled upon the hunchback in the dark. When he checked and learnt that the hunchback had no pulse, he thought that he had killed him. He propped the body against the wall of his neighbor's house to avoid blame.

The neighbor was a butler who always thought that the neighborhood dogs stole his butter. With a mallet in hand, he opened the door and found the hunchback against the wall. Thinking that it was actually a man who stole his butter, he struck the hunchback with the mallet. Looking at the lifeless body, the butler thought that he had killed the man. Afraid, he lifted the hunchback and left him in a dark alley.

As luck would have it, the sultan's broker was passing by. When he saw the hunchback in the dark alley, he mistook him for a thief. Angry, he struck him a blow. A watchman saw this and arrested him. The governor ordered the broker to be hanged as he had killed the hunchback.

When the executioner was about to hang the broker, the butler came forward and confessed how he had killed the hunchback with a mallet.

"Hang the butler!" the governor ordered. Just then the doctor came forward and confessed how he had stumbled upon the hunchback and killed him by accident.

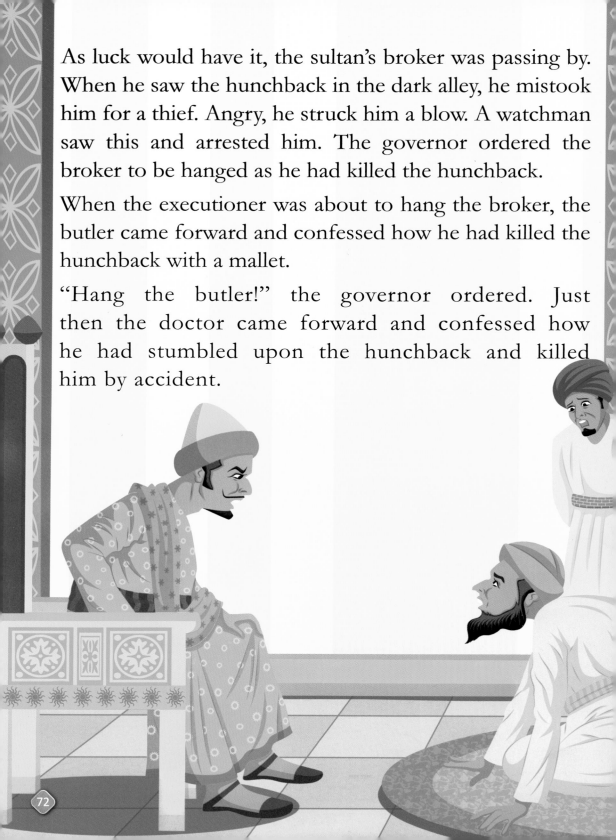

"Hang the doctor!" the governor ordered. Now the tailor came forward and confessed how the hunchback had choked on a fishbone at his table.

Hearing this, a barber requested the governor if he might examine the hunchback. Then, using pincers, he pulled out the fishbone from the hunchback's throat. The hunchback coughed and opened his eyes. He was not dead at all! Everyone admired the barber's quick-thinking. As everyone went their ways, the hunchback wondered what had conspired.

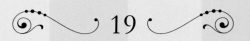

19

Golden Dreams

*T*here once lived in Baghdad a wealthy merchant named Farid. He lost all his money one day and became poor. He was not used to the life of being poor and started dreaming of becoming wealthy again.

One day, he dreamt that if he went to Cairo, he would become wealthy like before. He set out to fulfill his dream. Upon reaching Cairo, he took shelter in a mosque. At night when he was sleeping, some robbers robbed a neighboring house. When the guards came, they caught Farid thinking that he must be one of them.

When the judge asked Farid what he was doing in the mosque at night, Farid replied, "My dream has brought me to Cairo." On hearing Farid's fantastical story, the judge laughed at him. "You are a fool to chase dreams," he said. "I once dreamt of finding treasure in Baghdad but I did not pursue my dream."

Farid was excited, for Baghdad was his hometown. "I am from Baghdad, tell me more," he said.

"My dream told me to go to Baghdad and find a sand coloured house with red turrets," the judge said. "It further told me to look for a fountain in the garden of the house. Underneath the fountain was a buried treasure."

Finally, Farid was freed as the judge concluded that he was not a robber but a fool who chased dreams.

Now the house that the judge had described was Farid's. So the moment he was released, he returned to Baghdad. Digging underneath the fountain in his garden, he was surprised to find a box of jewels. Farid was no longer poor. The treasure box would last him a lifetime.

20

The Vizier and the Sage Duban

Once there lived a sultan named Yunan. He was suffering from a rare disease. None of his doctors could cure him.

Sage Duban, a seer, learnt that the sultan was suffering from leprosy. He went to the sultan's palace and informed the sultan that he could cure him. The grand vizier instantly became suspicious of Duban's intentions and forbade him to tend to the sultan in person. "Then I shall cure him without touching him," said Duban.

Sage Duban gifted the sultan a racket and asked him to play with it. He had cleverly put the medicine on the racket which got absorbed into the sultan's skin as he played with the racket.

Overnight, the sultan was cured of his illness. He was very pleased and showered the sage with precious gifts and money.

In time, the grand vizier grew jealous of Sage Duban's closeness to the sultan. He started filling sultan's ears, "O Sultan, if Duban can cure you without even touching you, he can also kill you the same way!" Sultan was weak, he easily believed his vizier and ordered his men to behead Duban.

On the day of his execution, Sage Duban presented sultan with a book and said, "This book contains all the knowledge of the world. It will guide you when I am no longer here."

When Duban had been executed, sultan opened the book but it was blank. Astonished, he started flipping the pages, licking his fingers to help him turn the pages quickly. The book was lined with poison and every time sultan licked his fingers, he consumed some of it. Soon, he lost his eye sight and fainted. If the sage was alive, the sultan would not have suffered so.